Eagle's Honour

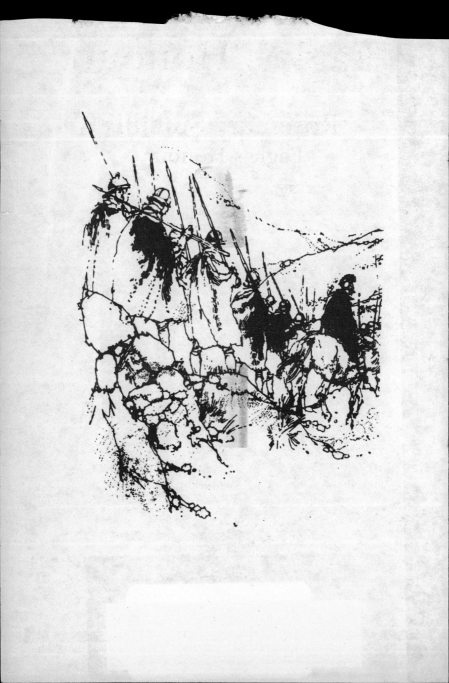

Eagle's Honour

Rosemary Sutcliff

RED FOX

A Red Fox Book

Published by Random House Children's Books
20 Vauxhall Bridge Road, London SW1V 2SA

A division of Random House UK Ltd
London Melbourne Sydney Auckland
Johannesburg and agencies throughout the world

A Circlet of Oak Leaves
Copyright © Text Anthony Lawton 1965, 1968
Copyright © Illustrations Victor Ambrus 1968

Eagle's Egg
Copyright © Text Anthony Lawton 1981
Copyright © Illustrations Victor Ambrus 1981

1 3 5 7 9 10 8 6 4 2

A Circlet of Oak Leaves first published in Great Britain 1965 by
Macmillan and Company Limited

Eagle's Egg first published in Great Britain 1981
by Hamish Hamilton Children's Books 1981

A Circlet of Oak Leaves and Eagle's Egg first published in
paperback in 1982 by The Hamlyn Publishing Group Limited

Red Fox edition 1995

Set in Baskerville by Intype, London
Printed and bound in Great Britain by
Cox & Wyman Ltd, Reading, Berkshire

RANDOM HOUSE UK Limited Reg. No. 954009

ISBN 0 09 935391 1

For
all four houses of
Hilsea Modern Girls' School, Portsmouth
(my school)
who adopted me like a battleship or a regimental goat

but just a little bit extra
for Sutcliff House

Contents

A Circlet of Oak Leaves

CHAPTER ONE

Outside, a little mean spring wind came siffling up from the river, humming across the parade ground of the great fortress in the dark, and tumbling the garbage along the narrow streets of Isca Silurium, but within the open door of the *Rose and Wine Skin* was lamplight and the warmth of braziers, and a companionable rise and fall of voices.

Three young Auxiliary Cavalrymen stood propped against the high trestle table at the far end, talking to the retired Gaulish Javelin man who kept the place, but each with an ear twitching towards the nearest corner, where a knot of Legionaries with long-service bracelets and faces like tanned harness leather, had pulled two benches together and were setting the world to rights.

'That's what I say!' One of the veterans brought an open hand down on the bench

beside him with a slam that set the wine cups jumping. 'All this talk about the need for more Cavalry is so much moon's-milk. It's *us*, the line-of-battle lads that carry the day, every time.'

Another nodded, consideringly. 'It's the speed and mobility they're after, of course.'

And a third laughed into his wine cup. 'Comes in useful for retreating.'

'It was just the same, that time the Picts broke through the Northern Wall – the time the Legate was killed. Six or seven wings of Cavalry, the 6th

12

had with them, when they went up to deal with that lot of blue painted devils, and so far as I can make out the Dacians were the only ones that didn't run like redshanks at the first sound of the Pictish yell.'

The young Auxiliaries had been listening to all this, staring straight before them. Now, one of them, flushing slowly crimson under his ragged cap of barley-pale hair, stepped out from the rest and edged over to the veterans.

'I ask pardon, sir,' he swallowed thickly. 'My mates and I couldn't help hearing. You did say, "As far as you could make out?" You weren't there yourself, then, sir?'

The first veteran looked up, his thick brows shooting towards the roots of his hair. 'No, I'd a brother there, if it concerns you. He lost a hand when the left flank was crumpled up – it helped him to remember.'

'I'm sorry, sir, but that – losing a hand, I mean – mightn't help him remember very clearly.'

One of the group gave a snort of laughter. 'It's a Cavalry cub. You've hurt his honour, Gavrus.'

'Too bad, Hirpinius,' Gavrus said. 'I've had enough of you, my lad. You're only a little boy, and you don't know anything yet but what the recruiting officer told you. Everyone knows the

Tungrians and the Asturians ran like redshanks.
Come back and quarrel with me when you've
learned to grow a beard!'

There was a roar of laughter from the rest of
the Legionaries. The boy's hands clenched into
large knuckled red fists. His mates had begun to
come up behind him. At any moment there was
going to be trouble, and the wine-shop owner

looked on anxiously. He had been an Auxiliary himself, and quite clearly, whatever happened, the boys were going to get the sticky end of the vine staff.

But at that moment a rangy, loose-limbed man, who had been lounging on the bench nearest the door, unfurled himself lazily and came across to join the group.

'The Picts fired the heather, and the flames stampeded the horses.'

Everyone turned to stare at him, including the shop's owner, who knew him well enough: head man to old Lyr the horse breeder, who came down a couple of times a year, with wild-eyed, rough-broken three-year-olds to sell to the garrison horse-master. And the man stared back at them out of slightly widened eyes that seemed pale as rain by contrast with his dark hard-bitten face.

Out of a moment's startled silence, Gavrus said, 'And who in Hades are you?'

'My name is Aracos, for what that's worth; from Thrace in the beginning, from the hills a day's trail westward now!'

'So. And it was fire that stampeded the horses?'

'Yes.'

15

'You were *there*, I suppose?'

'Yes.'

There was a general gasp, and somebody spluttered into his wine cup.

Then Gavrus, still only half believing, repeated, 'You *were* there?'

'I've lived long enough to be other things before I was a horse breeder.'

'Tungrian Cavalry? or Asturian?'

'Dacian,' Aracos said, and added obligingly, 'the ones who didn't run like redshanks, you know.'

Gavrus took a long swig at his wine, studying him over the rim of the cup all the while, then set it down. 'Oddly enough, I believe you. Just by way of interest, why *didn't* the Dacian horses stampede with the rest?'

'Because the Dacians teach their horses tricks. Haven't you ever seen a Dacian squadron showing off? Standing on horseback or clinging under the brute's belly, or leaping them through the flames of a fire-trench? When the Picts' fire came down on us, our horses were used to the flames, and not afraid.'

The young Auxiliaries looked at each other; one of them whistled under his breath.

'So simple as that, eh?' Abruptly Gavrus

shifted along the bench, his leathery face breaking into a grin. 'You've your cup with you – join us and fill up to show there's no ill feeling; you too, my bold infants. Hai, Landlord, more wine all round!' There was a general shifting up to make room, and in a few moments, the Auxiliaries still a little stiff, they were all sitting together, while the shop's owner himself brought the wine.

Pouring the harsh red stuff into the cup Aracos held out, he said, reproachfully, 'It must be four – five times you've been in here, and never said you were one of us.'

'You never asked me,' Aracos said.

Under the warming influence of the wine, the atmosphere was growing friendly, and Aracos felt the warmth of old comradeship and a familiar world drawing him in again, doing more, had he but realised it, than ever the rough Sabine wine could do, to make him unwary. . . .

They talked of girls, the price of barley-beer, the evil-mindedness of Centurions, and so came back again to old battles, to the one particular battle, ten years past.

One of the Legionaries, a dark-faced man more silent than his fellows, looked up abruptly

from the depth of his wine cup into which he had been staring. 'Of course! *That* was it!'

'Um?' Gavrus prompted.

'There was something else about that fight – I was trying to remember what it was.'

'And what was it?'

'One of the Auxiliaries earned himself the Corona Civica.'

'Sa ha! 'Tisn't often *that* goes to an Auxiliary. No offence, 'tisn't often it goes to anybody, come to that. Any idea who it was?'

'One of the fire-eating Dacians. I've an idea it was the pennant-bearer.' Hirpinius turned quickly to the stranger in their midst. 'Fools that we are! Of course you're the one who'd be knowing. . . .' He checked, his eyes suddenly widening at what he saw in Aracos's face, his mouth ajar.

But it was one of the Auxiliaries who said in a tone of awed discovery, 'It was you, wasn't it?'

The Corona Civica, the highest award for personal bravery under the Eagles! They were all staring at him now. 'You?' someone said incredulously. 'You!'

Something flickered far behind the horse breeder's eyes. For a moment he hesitated, then shrugged. 'You could say I earned it – yes.' There was a note of bitter amusement in his tone, as though he laughed inwardly at an ugly jest against himself.

'But man! Why keep it under your helmet! It isn't exactly a thing to be ashamed of!'

'I've no special reason to talk about it.'

'No reason – Oh, come on, lad, don't pretend you're not human.'

'See now,' Aracos said, 'I'm out from under the Eagles' Wings, and all that is in the past. A circle of gilt oak leaves doesn't carry any weight in the hill horse-runs. Let's drop it.'

But Gavrus, who seemed the leader among the rest, was already shouting for more wine to celebrate, and one of the Auxiliaries, who had been gazing worshipfully at the unsuspected hero in their midst, leaned forward and said, 'Sir – will you tell us about it?'

Aracos's face was flushed, and his pale eyes had reckless sparks in them, but at the eager words he set down his empty wine cup, which the moment before he had been holding up to be refilled with the rest, laughed, shook his head, and lounged a little unsteadily to his feet. 'Maybe another time – another year. Not tonight; I've an early start for the hills in the morning.'

Making his somewhat zigzag way back to the leather merchant's house on the outskirts of town where he always lodged when he brought the horses down, Aracos cursed inwardly by all the gods he knew.

What a fool he had been to get caught up in the thing at all. He must have been drunker than he realised. But in his inmost places he knew that drunk or sober would have made little difference. He couldn't have sat there and let the boys take up the challenge alone and land themselves in the trouble they were heading for.

Yes, but he might at least have had enough wits about him, when the Corona Civica came up, not to let the old story show all over his face. Ah well, it would be half a year before his next trip down from the hills; he'd probably never see tonight's bunch again, and old Sylvanus who kept the wine shop would forget.

CHAPTER TWO

But old Sylvanus did not forget. It made too good a story to tell to customers. Finally Aracos simply shrugged and accepted the situation. Being a hero was always good for a free drink, anyway.

He went on accepting it for two and a half years, and then one autumn day he went down to Isca Silurium with the usual string of remounts, struck his bargain with the garrison horse-master, and took himself to the *Rose and Wine Skin* to wash the dust of the horse-yards out of his throat.

Most of the men crowded about the braziers were strangers to him, but two or three Legionaries whom he knew were grouped together in the far corner. He headed across to join them, but mid-way, a voice exploded in his ear. 'Aracos! Now by Jupiter's Thunderbolt, if it isn't Aracos!' And as he looked round, somebody surged into his path; he saw a lean and beaky face with small bright eyes and a coarse, good-humoured mouth, and remembered it from a long time ago.

He felt as though someone had jolted him in the pit of the stomach. 'Nasik! What do you do here?' The words sounded stupid in his own ears.

'What should I be doing here? The Third Wing's just posted here – back from Pannonia. What do you do here?'

'Work for a Horse-Chieftain in the hills. Want any remounts?'

A couple of the older Cavalrymen joined in, grinning and exclaiming at the smallness of the Empire; the younger ones were new since his time. He had a choking desire to turn and thrust his way out into the street again, but that would not stop the thing happening, only mean it happening behind his back. . . .

And then old Sylvanus joined his voice to the rest. 'Here's a fine reunion. You'll have been together in that northern fighting, ten years ago? Well now, you're just the lads we want, for we've never yet got him to tell us how he came by the Corona Civica.'

A couple of the Legionaries whom Aracos

knew, had joined the group and added their voices to the rest. 'Now *you* can tell us. Come on now, tell the tale; don't be bashful, my wood anemone!'

Nasik looked from them to Aracos, puzzled; then burst into a shout of laughter. 'Corona Civica? It's a jest, isn't it?'

There was a sudden uneasiness among the onlookers, a sharp, startled pause. 'A jest? No, why should it be?' someone said.

Nasik broke off his laughter. 'You *don't* mean to say – did he tell you he got the Civica?'

Aracos stood quite still, fronting the perplexed and startled faces. There was a little smile on his mouth, as set as though it were carved in stone.

One of the Legionaries, as though defending himself in advance from the charge of being easily duped, said, 'One of the Dacians *did* get the Civica in that fight.'

'Yes, but not this one. Why, by our Lady of the Foals! He's never been a soldier! He was a medical orderly – an Army butcher's fetch-and-carry man!'

A second Dacian had come up beside the first. 'So you thought you'd snap up Felix's cast-off

glory, did you? He being dead and not needing it any more!'

The wine-shop owner turned a troubled eye on the silent man in their midst. 'Well? You'd best be saying something, hadn't you?'

The whole shop was silent to hear his answer, and Aracos, looking round at them with that lazy smile still engraved on his lips, saw that they were not exactly hostile – yet – but the startled perplexity was hardening into disgust, and a hint of the delight of boys watching a cat with a pannikin tied to its tail.

'Surely. It's all perfectly true,' he said on a note of amusement.

'But why?' – the wine-shop keeper began.

Aracos shrugged. 'It's dull, up in the hills. I wanted to see if you would be fools enough to believe me – and behold, you were.'

A growl of anger answered him, and a small red-haired Legionary got menacingly to his feet. 'Why you – you – I'll teach you to make fools of us again!'

But his neighbour seized him by the shoulder and slammed him back on to the bench. 'Leave him be. He's not worth getting rounded up by the Watch Patrol for, he looks a much worse fool than we do, anyway.'

Aracos turned to the landlord. 'I came in for a drink, but I don't much care for the smell in here tonight.' He turned, and pushed out into the windy dark, careful not to betray by the set of his shoulders that he heard the shout of laughter and the insults that followed him.

One man among the Dacians had looked up with a start when Nasik first shouted the new-comer's name, and had remained quite still, watching him, through the whole ugly scene that came after. In the somewhat shamefaced silence that followed the laughter, before the shout went up for more wine, he got up with some excuse to his companions, and left the wine shop.

Outside in the street he checked a moment, then turned uphill towards the Dexter Gate of the fortress, still dimly visible in the gusty autumn twilight.

Aracos went downhill towards his lodging. He would not think until he got back to the little room under the roof where he could be alone. He must get away from people, from faces in the light of open doorways.

He came to the leather merchant's door and went in. The daughter of the house came out from an inner room when she heard him; he had always liked her, but tonight he only wanted to be left alone. 'You are early,' she said, 'but supper will be ready soon.'

He shook his head. 'I am not hungry, Cordaella.'

He went past her, up the ladder to the room under the roof. He kicked the door shut behind him, and sat down on the narrow cot. The small earthenware lamp had been lit ready for him, early though he was, and he sat staring at it, not seeing it at all, seeing only the faces in the *Rose and Wine Skin*, hearing the laughter. He wouldn't come down to Isca Silurium again. Old Lyr could make some other arrangement about getting his horses sold. The small sharp pain that came on him sometimes after an especially hard struggle with an unbroken colt, was flickering under his ribs and down his left arm, but he was no more aware of it than he was of the lamp flame.

CHAPTER THREE

A long while later, feet came up the ladder, and a hand was on the latch. Cordaella's voice said, 'Aracos.'

'Go away, Cordaella. I'm not hungry.'

'There is someone here to speak with you.'

'Tell whoever it is,' Aracos said carefully and distinctly, 'to go to Gehenna!'

There was a murmur of voices. The latch rattled down, the door opened and closed again. 'I am sorry,' said a quiet voice. 'Don't blame the woman; she tried to stop me.'

Aracos swung round to see a slight youngish man with the badge of the Dacian Horse on his belt buckle, and on the breast of his tunic the entwined serpents of Esculapius that marked him for one of the Medical Corps. Aracos had not consciously noticed him in the wine shop, but he knew him again.

'Get out!'

'Presently.'

'Now! Didn't you have enough fun in the *Rose and Wine Skin* that you must come after me for more?'

'I would have been here sooner.' The young Medic ignored that. 'But had to go back to my quarters to fetch this that I have for you – from Felix.'

'Felix is dead,' Aracos said dully. 'I didn't know, until they said so this evening.'

'He died between my hands, two years ago in Pannonia. He bade me take this, and get it to a certain Aracos from Thrace, who was a medical orderly with the Dacians during the Pictish troubles. But you had left the Eagles, and I could not pick up your trail, so I have kept it with my own gear ever since, just on the chance. . . .' He bent and laid on the cot a flat bundle wrapped in a piece of old uniform cloth. 'The Empire is a small place, as our friends said.'

Aracos took up the bundle and slowly folded back the tattered cloth. Inside was a battered circlet of gilded bronze fashioned into the form of oak leaves. The Corona Civica!

'He said it was yours by rights.'

Aracos was silent for a few moments, holding

the thing gently between his hands. 'How did he die?'

'Of wounds taken in driving off an attack on the supply train he was escorting. It was three days later, before he got them into camp. The Gods know how he kept going so long.'

In the silence the wind gusted against the house, and sent a rustling charge of dry leaves along the court outside.

'I had a feeling,' the young Medic said at last, 'that you could have said something in your own defence, tonight, and that you deliberately chose to hold it back.'

'Did you?' Aracos said, without interest.

He was remembering how it had all begun, the day when he had gone down from his village in the Rhodope Mountains with two other lads, to the recruiting station at Abdera. He could sit a horse with anyone, and it had not occurred to him that the small sharp pain that sometimes caught him in the chest after running uphill was anything to keep him out of the Thracian Cavalry. At Abdera a man with entwined serpents on the breast of his tunic had made each of them in turn run to the sacred olive tree half a mile away and back without stopping, and then

laid his ear against their chests and listened to something inside. The other two had been accepted, but not Aracos, though he had run faster than either of them. He wondered later if the man had heard the small pain in his chest that the running had given him.

He hadn't gone home, he would have been shamed, but he found that there was room for other men than warriors under the Eagles, jobs for which you did not have to have anyone listening to your chest. He had liked the man with the entwined serpents, and he was interested by this running and listening; he wanted to know what you could hear inside people that told you they had a pain. And so he had become a medical orderly, with the Thracians at first, then with the Dacian Horse in the far-off province of Britain.

He remembered the great outpost fort of Trimontum on the skirts of its three-peaked hill. He remembered Felix at Cavalry manoeuvres, Felix in his pennant-bearer's wolfskin, riding full tilt at the head of the flying squadron, with the long sleeve-pennant of scarlet silk filling with the wind and streaming from its silver serpent-head on the lance point. It was just at the end of those manoeuvres that the youngster had been

thrown and broken his collar bone; but for that they would probably never have even spoken to each other, for clerks and orderlies and such, Aracos had very soon discovered, were in the Legions and Auxiliaries, but not *of* them. The odd thing was that they were very much alike save that Felix was not so dark, so that for all the seven or eight years difference between them, old Diomedes the camp surgeon called them Castor and Pollux, when Felix came to have his shoulder tended.

He remembered news of unrest filtering down from the north at the end of a long dry summer, the smoke signals feathering the sky; the Dacian Wings under those slim scarlet serpent pennants riding out to join the 6th Legion on its forced march northward. He remembered following with the baggage carts in the dust of the marching columns, the heather swimming in the heat, the Pictish harrying that began on the second day; a wolf-pack worrying along their flanks, nightly attacks, scouting patrols that came back bloody and at half strength – one that never came back at all.

He remembered the last night, the knowledge on them all that full battle was coming with the morning; the ordered stir of the camp that never

died down all through the tense hours of
darkness.

CHAPTER FOUR

In the first ghost-grey light before a misty dawn, Aracos went down to the latrine trenches beyond the horse lines (the Legions never camped a night without digging such trenches and setting up a stockade) and found Felix there, his wolf-skin flung behind him, being violently sick.

'Felix! What is it?'

And then as the boy crouched back on his heels and turned a sweat-streaked face to him, he knew. Felix's squadron had run into trouble more than once during the forced march north, and lost several men; the last time, he had got back with a friend's body slung across his horse's withers, a body with part of the face carried away by a throw-spear, that had still been alive when they set out on the struggle back to camp. That had been once too often.

'Aracos!' The boy was shaking from head to foot, and his teeth chattered as though he had

a fever. 'Aracos! Thank the Gods it's you! Help me—'

Aracos caught his shoulders to steady him. 'You're the only one who can do that.'

'*You* can – you *can*.'

'How?'

'There must be something. The German

Berserks chew leaves of some sort, don't they?'
He was beyond shame; that would come later.
'I'd get drunk, but it only makes me sleepy.' He
bent his face into his hands.

'Stop it!' Aracos said. 'You can! I've known
men as sick as a cat in the dawn and fight like
tigers an hour later.'

But when the other looked up again, he knew
that he was wrong; he had served with the Eagles
long enough to know the look on the face of a
man who had reached the end of what he could
take. Now, what in the name of Night's Daugh-
ters was to be done? Whatever it was, it must be
done quickly.

Scarcely realising what he did, he caught up
the wolfskin and dragged the boy to his feet,
and an instant later was crouching with him
behind the long mound of earth turned up by
the trench diggers. 'Listen – I can't give you
anything; I can't and I won't!' Then as Felix
made a convulsive movement, 'No *listen*; there's
only one way out – we're about the same size,
and like enough to pass in the dust of fighting.
Strip off those leathers.'

'You mean you—'

'Yes.' Aracos was already yanking at a shoulder
buckle.

'You can't.'

'I've got to, haven't I? Quick now, off with your breeks.' Felix obeyed him, but his eyes had a strange blankness, as though he did not hear. Aracos snatched the breeks from him and dragged them on. 'Where's your horse.'

Felix's gaze turned on him with the same blankness.

'Your horse! Where's he picketed?'

'The end of the second line.'

'Right.' He had the tunic on now, belt, sword belt, the great wolfskin with the head pulled well forward on his brows. 'I'm away now. Don't follow for a hundred heart-beats. Then make for the baggage park, lie up in one of the tilt carts nearest to the stockade until I come back, and pray to the Gods, for your own sake as well as mine, that I *do* come back. I'll whistle "The Girl I Kissed at Clusium". Don't move until you hear the tune.'

The young pennant-bearer still seemed in a daze, but he could not wait to make sure he understood. All he could do was to take the youngster's place and hope for a miracle to bring them both through the day without disaster.

Looking back, he still did not know whether

he had done right, he only knew that at the time there had seemed nothing else that he could do, and that the miracle had happened. In the ordered bustle of the camp, with the watch fires turning sickly and scarcely a finger of light in the sky, he had got through the issue of food, collected the serpent pennant from its place with the Cohort Colours and the Eagle itself before the Legate's tent. He had seen it done so often that he made no obvious mistake in the ceremonial; and at half-light, with morning mist thickening among the hills, found himself riding, still unrecognised, behind the Captain at the head of the two wings of Dacian Horse.

The manoeuvring for position, the coming and going of Scouts, the hurried Councils of War in the Legate's tent, belonged to yesterday, and he had known nothing of them anyway; his business in life was the medical supplies, not the tactics of hill warfare. And now, as they rode down into the steep river valley across the narrows of which the Tungrians had been standing to all night, and took up their position in reserve behind the steadily forming battle line, his business was with the light sleeve of scarlet silk lifting and stirring from the lance shaft in his hand; to carry out the pennant-bearer's duties with no betraying mistake, and to keep his face hidden.

The rising mist was warm and milky, no freshness in it. The waiting seemed interminable.

And then far ahead, a flurry of shouting broke the silence, and all along the battle line and the ranks of the Reserves ran a tiny ripple of the nerve ends, like an unheard touch on the taut strings of a harp. Somewhere out in front the Roman outposts were already engaged. The

shouting came nearer; Pictish war horns were snarling in the mist and the Roman trumpets crowed in answer. And now, to the shouting, was added a clanging and clashing and an earth-shaking rumble that Aracos had heard before, but never from the fighting-ranks, and out of the mist swept a column of war chariots, driven and manned by naked, blue-painted warriors.

They swept across the Roman front, raining down throw-spears which the Legionaries caught for the most part on their shields, and wheeling about on the steepening skirts of the hillside, would have cut in between the first rank and the second. But the Cretan archers posted between the Asturian squadrons on the left flank, wheeled half left as they passed, and loosed a flight of short arrows into their midst, aiming for the teams rather than the men. Team after team came down in kicking chaos and a rending crash of broken yoke-poles and torn-off wheels; the charge lost shape and impetus, and swung away, straightening itself back into some kind of order as it went; and from farther to the right, another column came screaming down upon the Roman battle line. The mist was growing ragged before the light breeze that had begun to wake with the dawn, and a brief gleam of light from

the rising sun slid into the eyes of the archers
on the right wing, making their aim less sure; a
team went down here and there, but the wild
head of the column was into the Tungrian Cavalry before they could be stopped, and in the

same instant, from dead ahead, a wave of foot-warriors came yelling out of the mist and flung themselves upon the pilums of the main battle line. The pilums drank blood, but there seemed always more, where the first wave had come from.

Aracos, in his place in the Reserve, the slim scarlet banner hanging limp from the lance-shaft in his hand, was never clear about what happened then. All that his mind kept of the battle, afterwards, was a memory of roaring chaos, until suddenly, unbelievably, the trumpets were sounding for Advance and Follow-Up, and he realised with a leap of the heart, that the Picts were falling back.

The whole struggle was moving north-westward up the curve of the valley. Close behind him, the Dacian Captain snapped an order, and the Cavalry trumpets were yelping. Felix's horse, as though catching the surge of excitement, flung up his head with a shrill squeal, and buckled forward under his new rider. But it was not yet fighting time for the Reserves. They only moved forward, keeping station behind the reeling battle line, over dead and wounded men.

The northward surge of the battle slowed and checked once, as though the Picts were making a desperate stand, then rolled on again. The valley swung farther west, rising underfoot, the mist was growing more and more ragged, and suddenly it rolled away like a curtain, still clinging to the northern side of the valley but leaving clear the sheer heather slopes to the south, where a great spur of rock and scree jutted out almost to overhang the narrowing glen.

The man beside him shouted, 'Mithras! Look up there!' and following his wildly pointing finger, Aracos saw the crest of the spur swarming with Painted Men. They were prising loose stones out of the heather, and at that very instant the first of these, flung by a naked giant, came whizzing down with the power of a ballista bolt, and somewhere among the surging mass of Legionaries a man screamed – half a scream. But a far worse menace was the great boulder, already perilously poised, that topped the crag, round which the Painted Men were labouring with deadly purpose. There were lesser stones to be hauled from about its base, and spear butts made flimsy levers for shifting such a huge mass, but Aracos saw with a sickening lurch of the heart that it was only a matter of time before that vast boulder came crashing down into the midst of the Roman battlemass, bringing with it, by the look of things, half the hillside as it came.

The Eagles had been led into a trap!

Ahead, the Legionary trumpets were sounding, fiercely urgent. They were echoed by the light notes of the Cavalry trumpets, and three squadrons of Asturians broke away and headed

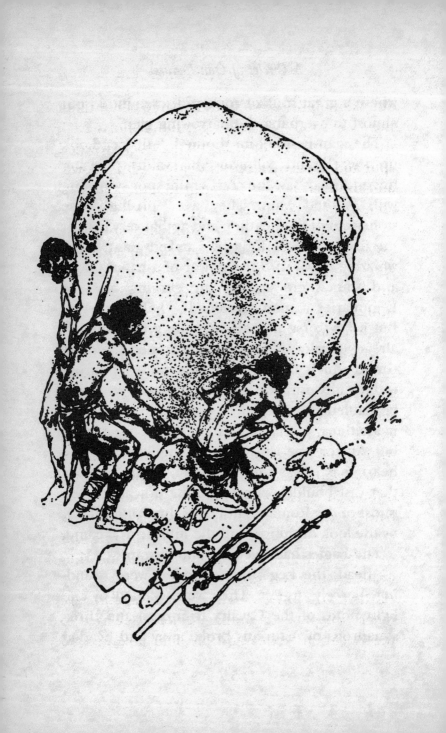

at a slant up the steep hillside, while below them the Centurions fought to get the Cohorts back from the deadly menace of the rock-crowned spur and the great stones already crashing down, and the Pictish warrior-swarm fought as desperately to pen them in.

Suddenly out of the low sunlight leapt flame that danced up just below the hill shoulder, and spread from point to point into a single curved line of fire, red in the daylight, rippling and undulating towards the horsemen.

'Gods! They've fired the heather!'

In the face of the fire across their path, the Asturians' horses balked and wheeled about, snorting in terror, and flung back from the flames, those in front spreading instant confusion among those behind, and the whole lot, for all the efforts of their riders to check and turn them, stampeding away downhill like unbroken colts. And now the horses on the battle-wings were catching the smell of the fire and the terror of their own kind, flinging this way and that. A few moments more and they would be utterly unmanageable.

'Right! It's us now!' The Dacian Captain gave quick orders to his message-rider: 'Get back to the Decurian Sextus and bid him take Second

Wing and the hind four squadrons of First forward to hold the battle flank. The rest of First Wing – *With Me*!'

Trumpets yelped again. Aracos drove his heel into the bay's flank and was away at the Captain's side; the wind of their going took the thin scarlet silk and the body of the serpent pennant filled and rippled out, as he set his horse at the slope, the rest drumming at their heels. Smoke wafted into his eyes, sparks and wisps of burning heather were breaking free and drifting ahead of the main blaze, little red tongues licking up wherever they landed; the thin wall of fire, leaping high now in the morning breeze, rippled like the thin red serpent silk, bending over as though to greet and engulf them. Aracos felt the bay brace and gather himself under him, then hold straight on, not swerving from the flames ahead. Let the Tungrians laugh in future at the Dacians' tricks!

At the last instant the Captain gave a great shout, then with his cloak flung across nose and mouth, plunged straight into the wall of flame. Aracos galloped at his side, face driven down into the wolfskin. Hideous, blasting heat lapped him round, not a wall of flame, but a whole world of flame. He choked into the wolfskin as

pain tore at his eyes and throat and lungs – then they were through. There was a stink of singeing horsehide, sparks hung in the rough wolfskin and in the horse's mane, a fringe of flame lengthened the tail of the scarlet serpent. Ahead, the blackened and smoking hillside rose to the spur

where the Painted Men still laboured savagely about the great tottering boulder. But away to the right, something moved under cover of the smitch, and next instant a flurry of javelins and sling-stones took the Dacians on the flank. Men and horses went down. Still riding hard for the spur, Aracos was aware of the Captain swaying beside him, clutching at the shaft of a javelin that stuck out from under his collar-bone – choking to him a last order to take them on and clear the spur, before he pitched down among the horses' hooves.

So he took them on, through a vicious squall of slingstones. Where the ground grew too steep to ride they dropped from the horses and ran on, crouching with heads down behind their light bronze-rimmed bucklers. By the time they reached the spur, hearts and lungs bursting within them, he had no idea how many or how few were still behind him; he had had no chance to look round. He did not even know that many of the horses, lightened of their riders' weight, had come scrambling after them, bringing their own weapons, the stallions' weapons of teeth and trampling hooves, into the fight. He only knew that the time came when there were no more Painted Men left alive on the spur, and that the terrible boulder, swaying as it seemed to every breath, was still there.

They jammed loose stones under it, and added a few war-painted bodies for good measure, but to Aracos it was all hazy, and the

only thing that seemed quite real was the pain in his chest that spread all down his shield-arm and made a buzzing darkness before his eyes. He fought the darkness off. If he collapsed now they would pull off the wolfskin to find where he was wounded, and see his face. But he never afterwards had the least idea how they got back to the main force, nor how the rest of that day went, save that somehow, incredibly, it ended in a Roman victory, dragged out of what had nearly been the most hideous defeat.

When things began to seem real again, he was back in camp, and tending Felix's bay, who had a spear gash in his flank and looked, like his neighbours in the picket lines, to have been ridden hard all day. There was a vague half-memory in him of having been hunting – not deer or wild ox, but painted men among the heather; and a rather clearer one of setting a wisp of scorched scarlet silk on a lance shaft back in the row of Colours before the Legate's tent.

In the dusk and the ordered confusion, it was not hard to slip away unnoticed, but it could not be long before the cry went up for the pennant-bearer of the Dacian Horse. With the wolfskin stripped off and rolled into an unbetraying bundle under one arm, he made for the baggage park, and slipped in among the carts nearest to the stockade. The pain in his chest came and went, like a beast flexing its muscles to spring. He leaned against a wheel, and whistled softly, as well as he could for lack of breath, the first bars of 'The Girl I Kissed at Clusium'.

There was no answering whistle, but as he listened, something stirred in the next cart. He went to it quickly, and pulling himself up, peered under the tilt.

'Felix!'

Among the sacks and bales, something stirred again, and the pale blur of a face swam in the gloom. 'All's over,' he whispered, 'and all's well. Out now – they'll be missing you at any moment.'

'Aracos! Oh, thank the God's you're back! I was – so afraid you would go down.'

'For your sake, or mine?' Aracos said grimly, and then, 'Na, forget I said it. Get these on and out with you and take over your empty place. They've killed the Captain. Remember you led First Wing up to clear the Painted People from a hill spur where they were heaving rocks down on the Legion. They fired the heather, but you got through. There's a singed place on the flank of the wolfskin, you'd best rub your face in it.'

He was dragging off the leather breeks as he spoke, and tossed them into the cart after tunic and wolfskin. He heard an inarticulate sound that was almost a sob. The boy had lain there all day, alone with himself, and the Mother of Foals alone knew what kind of shape he was in now, to carry the thing through; but he could not wait to see. The beast in his chest was getting ready to spring, and he must get clear of the baggage park while he could.

There was a high sweet ringing in his ears, and black webs spun between his eyes and the camp fires, as he turned away towards the wattle shelters beyond a knot of hawthorn scrub where the Medics would be busy with the wounded. He must have been missed, of course; he must think of some reason to give, some story to tell that would not turn anyone's thoughts towards the Dacians' pennant-bearer. . . . He was quite close to one of the fires when the beast in his chest leapt. He took one more step, choking for air against the rending teeth and claws, and had just sense and time left to turn towards the fire as he stumbled to his knees. The black webs spun into solid darkness as he sank forward on to his face among the hot ash. His last thought was that at least the marks of fire on him would be accounted for.

When the darkness ebbed again, he was lying on his back with men standing round him, and one kneeling over him with an ear pressed to his chest, just as the man had done who turned him down for the Thracian Horse.

'He just loomed up out of the darkness and

went head first into the fire,' someone said. 'Has he been at the barley spirit?'

'No,' said the man with an ear to his chest, and the voice was that of Diomedes, the surgeon. Then, straightening up, 'Poor brute, he must have felt it coming on him and hidden away like a sick animal.'

Another voice pointed out, 'You heard what these men said; he hasn't just been lying around here all day, sir.'

'I said hidden away, not lying around. I imagine he thought the worst was over, and was on his way back to duty when it took him again.'

In the end, they had decided that he had some sort of rift in his heart that the strain of the campaign had worsened, and he was invalided out with a small sickness gratuity, just about the time the news came through that Felix had won the Corona Civica for clearing the Picts from the hill spur after the Wing Captain was killed, and thereby most likely saving the Legion.

They had been back at Trimontum leaving the north quiet behind them, a good while by then, and Aracos was going south next day with a returning supply train; south, and out from the service of the Eagles.

Felix had hunted him out, where he had gone down the river glen to make a last small sacrifice at the Altar to Fortune which one of the garrison had put up long ago. The boy looked old and haggard, as though he were the one who had been ill. 'I cannot go through with this!' he said desperately.

'Yes, you can.'

'I *can't*! I'm going to tell them. I don't care what they do to me, anything would be better than this!'

And Aracos had caught him by the shoulders as he had done once before. 'Now listen! The Gods know why I was fool enough to do what I did for you, but this I know; you're not going to undo it all now!'

There had been a long silence, broken only by the voice of the little stream that flowed out from under the shrine, and then Felix had moaned softly, like something with a physical hurt. 'I could hack myself to pieces! I don't know what happened and I don't know it won't happen again. . . . If only I could be the one to pay. . . .'

Aracos had tightened his grip. 'You'll pay your share, all right. All your life you're going to have to wear that circlet of gilded oak leaves through

your shoulder-strap, and feel men's eyes on it, and know the truth behind it. Oh, you'll pay, Felix, so we can cry quits.'

And he had seen the slack despairing lines of the boy's face tauten, and his head go up, as he took the strain.

'But what will you do?' he asked after a while.

'Stay on in Britain. I spent my first year in the province on garrison duty at Burrium. There's good horse country among the Welsh hills. I might try to get work there. I've my gratuity; I shan't starve while I'm looking for it.'

CHAPTER FIVE

A whirling moth blundered into the lamp flame, and fell away, singed and sodden, and Aracos was in the present again. He was alone, though he had not heard the young Medic go, and still holding between his hands the battered circlet of gilded oak leaves. In one place the bronze showed through, where the gilt was all rubbed away by the shoulder-strap through which it had been worn for more than eight years.

Again he remembered Felix's set face. Oh yes, Felix had paid his price. And in the end – what had the Medic said? 'He died between my hands, two years ago in Pannonia . . . of wounds taken in driving off an attack on the supply train he was escorting. It was three days later, before he got them into camp. The Gods know how he kept going so long.'

A small inward bitterness that had been with Aracos for ten years suddenly fell away. He had

been worth saving, that boy. He thought with a
detached interest, as though it concerned somebody else and not himself at all, that now he
could tell the truth, and be believed. But the
thought remained detached. One didn't betray
a friend merely because he was dead.

But he knew, for no very clear reason, that
because that wild day's work ten years ago had

not been wasted, because Felix had died in the way he had done, and dying, had sent him the battered circlet of oak leaves, he would bring down the remounts again next spring, and go to the *Rose and Wine Skin* again – and again – and again, until the story grew too threadbare to be bothered with any more, and he had come out beyond it.

He folded the Corona Civica carefully in its bit of old cloth again, and getting up, opened the door and called down the ladder, 'Cordaella! Is there any supper left?'

Eagle's Egg

CHAPTER ONE

The Girl at the Well

All right then, if it's a story you're wanting, throw another log on the fire. The winters strike colder now than they used to do when I was a young man in Britain: and I'll tell you. . . .

Eburacum was a frontier station in my father's day; your great-grandfather's. But Roman rule spread northward in one way and another; and by the time I was posted up there as Eagle Bearer to the Ninth Legion it wasn't a frontier station any more, and the settlement that had gathered itself together under the fortress walls had become a sizeable town, with a forum where the business of the place was carried on, and wine shops, and temples to half a score of different gods.

Well, so I was ambling up the narrow, crooked street behind the temple of Sulis on one of those dark edge-of-spring evenings when it seems as though all the colour has drained out of the

world and left only the grey behind. I was off
duty and I was bored. I'd been down at the lower
end of the town to look at some new young
fighting cocks that Kaeso had for sale, but I
hadn't liked the look of any that he had shown
me, and taking it all in all, I was feeling
thoroughly out at elbows with the world. And
then I rounded the corner of the temple garden;
and there, at the well that bubbled up from
under the wall, a few paces further up the street,
a girl was drawing water. And I knew I'd been
wrong about there being no colour left in the
world, because her hair lit up that grey street
like a dandelion growing on a stubble pile. –
No, that's not right either, it was redder and
more sparkling; a colour that you could warm
your hands at. And the braids of it, hanging
forward over her shoulders 'thick as a swords-
man's wrist' as the saying goes.

You can guess the next bit, I dare say. Up I
strolled, and stood beside her, and gave her my
best smile when she turned round.

'That pail is much too heavy for a little bird
like you,' said I. 'Better let me carry it for you.'

She stood and looked at me out of the bluest
and brightest eyes I'd ever seen in any girl's
head; not smiling back, but as though something

amused her, all the same: and I got the feeling that I was not the first of our lads who had offered to carry her bucket home for her from the well of Sulis.

'It is not, really,' she said, 'and I am quite used to it.'

' "Never carry your own bucket if you can find somebody else to carry it for you". That's what we say in the Legions, more or less,' I told her. And I picked up the brimming pail from where she had set it on the well curb, and stood ready to carry it wherever she wanted.

'Then – that is our house, yonder at the bend of the street,' she said. 'The one with the workshop beside it and the big blue flower painted on the wall.'

And the laughter was still in her, because I had hoped it was much further off than that; and she knew it.

I should have to make the most of the little distance there was. I walked as slowly as possible, making a great show of not spilling the water, and said, 'Why have I not seen you before? With that bonny brightness of hair I couldn't have missed you.'

'I do have a cloak with a hood to it,' she said. And then, stopping her teasing. 'But indeed I

have not been long in Eburacum. My brother is making the picture-floor in the new Council Chamber, and he brought me up with him from Lindum, because he thinks that a growing town like this would be a good place for a craftsman to settle.'

And then we had reached the door, and I put the pail down, and she thanked me. We stood for an instant looking at each other, and an odd thing happened. We both turned shy.

'Do you go to the well at the same time every day?' I managed at last.

And she said, 'Most days, yes,' already picking up the bucket.

'Maybe we'll meet there again, some time—' I began. But before I could finish, she had gone in, and the door was quietly and gently shut in my face.

I did not even know her name.

Well, I could probably get that from her brother if I went along to the Council Chamber and admired his floor. I had seen and spoken with him more than once already. No problem there. But the girl had not really gone deep with me, yet, and I strolled back to the fortress thinking about the Council House and the things that had led up to it.

It was just about a year since the General Agricola had come out from Rome with orders to bring Caledonia, away north of us, within the frontiers of the Empire. He had taken the Second and Fourteenth Legions and pushed up through South Western Caledonia, and pegged down the country with a handful of forts and marching camps. – A friend of mine who was with the Second at the time told me it was pretty dull: not much serious fighting because the local tribes didn't know how to combine and seemingly hadn't found a leader strong enough to hammer them into one war-host.

At summer's end, when Agricola came back out of the wilds, he let it be known that there would be help from the Treasury for any town that liked to smarten itself up, with a new bathhouse, say, or a council chamber or a triumphal arch. Somehow he'd got it into the heads of the local chiefs that it was beneath their dignity to live in towns that looked like broken-down rookeries, while in the south of Britain the people had public buildings that Rome herself would not be ashamed of. So architects and craftsmen were got up from the south and back in the autumn Eburacum had started building a fine new Council Chamber.

It had been a mild winter, and so the work had gone forward most of the time, and by winter's end most of the work was done and the thick fluted roof tiles were in place, so that the floor could be begun. A real Roman picture-floor that was to be the chief glory of the place. In the early days the Elders had meant to bring in a Roman artist. But after a while, when the money began to run short, they had had to shorten their ideas to match.

And so came Vedrix, up from Lindum, instead. I've always been interested in seeing how things are made; and so, as I say, I'd already got into the way of wandering along sometimes, when I was off-duty, to watch him at work with his hammer and chisel, cutting his little cubes of chalk and sandstone, and brick and blue shale, and fitting them together into his picture.

A fiery little runt of a man, he was, with a white bony face that changed all the time, and hair like a bunch of carrots – and that's an odd thing, too, because later, when I saw him and his sister together, their hair was the same colour; and yet hers never made me think of a bunch of carrots – and a lame leg that he told me once had mended short after he broke it when he was a boy. But he was the kind of artist-

craftsman who could turn his hand to most things and make a good job of them. So later on, when that floor was finished, it was a pretty good floor on the whole, though I still think the leopard looked a bit odd. But I suppose when you remember that he had never seen a real one, and had only a painted leopard on a cracked wine jar to copy, the wonder is that it didn't look odder still.

But, I'm getting ahead of myself. The picture-floor was only just a few days begun when I first saw my red-haired girl at the Well of Sulis. I spent a good deal of my free time watching it grow in the next few days also, for I'd found Vedrix an interesting fellow to talk to before I knew he was brother to the bonniest girl in all Eburacum, I certainly didn't find him less interesting afterwards.

CHAPTER TWO

Marching Orders

I didn't ask him her name, though. Somehow I found I didn't want to ask that of anyone but herself. So I waited, and for quite a while I was not off duty at the right time again. But at last the waiting was over, and we both chanced together once more at the Well of Sulis; and I carried her pail home for her again; and that time we got as far as telling each other our names on the door-sill.

'Now that we've met again, we should know each other's names,' I said. 'Mine is Quintus, what is yours?'

'Cordaella,' she said, tucking in the ends of her hair that were being teased out by the wind.

'That's a beautiful name,' said I. 'It fits you.'

And suddenly she laughed at me. 'So I have been told.' And she ran inside and shut the door on me again.

Then the day came when I had the sneezing fever.

'Do they not give you anything for that, up at the fort?' she said.

I had a sudden picture inside my head, of myself going up on Sick Parade, to bother Manlius the fort surgeon with my snufflings, and what he would say if I did. And that made me laugh so much despite my aching head, that I started coughing again, and leant against the doorpost choking and sneezing enough to put any girl off me for life. But she turned suddenly kind, and said, 'Come you in to the fire, and I will give you something. I have some herb skill, even if your fat fort surgeon has none.'

And she brought me in and sat me down by the fire on the central hearth of the warm smoky house-place; and she set the old slave-woman who came out of the shadows at her call, to heating water in a little bronze pot over the flames, while she herself fetched herbs and a lump of honeycomb from some inner place; and when they had boiled all together, she poured the brew off into a cup and gave it to me, saying, 'Now, drink – as hot as you can.'

So, more to please her than for any faith I had in it, I sipped and snuffled my way through

the scalding brew. It was sweet with the honey and greasy with the melted comb-wax, and the smoke of all the nameless herbs that had gone into it seemed to go right to the back of my nose and drift around inside my skull, so that for a moment I thought the top was coming off my head. But in a little it began to ease the aching, and truly I think that I began to mend from that moment.

Aye well, in one way and another, we contrived to see quite a bit of each other as that spring drew on. And after a while I kissed her, and she kissed me back as sweet as a hazel-nut. But it was after we had kissed each other, that we began to be unhappy. More and more unhappy. I daresay that sounds odd and the wrong way round, but we had our reasons, – seeing that the Legions don't allow any marrying 'below the vine staff'; below the rank of Centurion, that is.

'Maybe you will get promotion,' Cordaella said again and again.

But I wasn't very hopeful. It seemed to me that what I wanted was so tremendous that the Gods would surely never give it to me. 'Maybe,' I said, 'and maybe not. Anyway it will not be for a long time, and your brother has other plans for you. You told me so yourself.'

'There are two words as to my brother's plans,' said Cordaella, with a sniff. But there could be no sniffing at the Legion's rule about marrying below the vine staff.

I went round by the new Council Chamber on my way back to barracks, to have a word with Vedrix. I hadn't much idea what I was going to say to him, but there might be something; and anyway it was better than not saying or doing anything at all.

I heard the light tapping of his little hammer before I came in from the forecourt, and there he was squatting among his sticks of shale and sandstone, cutting them up into fine pavement cubes and setting them in place in the pattern. He was working on the ivy-leaf border, and I did not interrupt him; just stood looking, until he came to a good stopping place and sat back on his heels and grinned up at me like a fox.

'Odd to think of our Elders sitting here solemnly in their Roman tunics and on carved Roman chairs, to settle the affairs of the city. Not so long ago, when there was any settling to be done, the chiefs gathered to the council fire, and sat on their spread bulls'-hides with their weapons left outside.'

'Ever so civilised it's getting in these parts,' I said.

He shrugged. 'So the noble General Agricola would have us believe. If we are busy enough being Roman and civilised, we shall not notice that we are only strengthening our own bondage.'

There was a sudden harsh silence, and then I heard my own voice saying, 'You mind, don't you? I did not think that you minded.'

'Because I make a picture-pavement for the Romans and the British-Romans?' he said; and then, carefully fitting another cube into its place, 'How should I not mind that Rome rules me and my people, who have been free?'

'I don't know,' I floundered a bit. 'I suppose I thought – well, artists and poets and such don't seem to mind so much about who actually holds the rule, so long as they can get on with making their statues or their songs as they like.'

Vedrix set another little cube in place, settling it down with his round-nosed mallet. 'We of the Tribes,' he said, 'we don't divide people up, as you Romans do, into neat bundles – soldiers or tent-makers or wine merchants or poets. I'd have been out with the fighting men in the Troubles three years since, but for this short leg of mine.

– I can handle a spear as well as most, but I'm slow on the hills, and that makes a man dangerous to his comrades.'

'I'm sorry,' I said awkwardly.

He turned a cube of blue shale over in his fingers, and bent to settle it in place. 'You have no need to be,' he said, very carefully.

'No,' I stumbled, 'not about that. – I'm sorry I got it wrong about tent-makers and poets.' I felt the whole conversation getting away from me, and certainly getting further every moment from what I had come to talk to him about. I took a deep breath, and swallowed, 'Vedrix,' I said, 'I want to talk to you seriously about something, and you're making it all more and more difficult.'

'So? I am listening. Speak then, as seriously as you please.'

Somehow, almost without knowing it, I slipped into the British tongue, the Celtic tongue. I had grown used to speaking it, after a fashion, with Cordaella, for the Celtic is better than the Latin, for making love-talk to a British girl, and easier for explaining to her brother in, too.

I said, 'The love is upon me, for Cordaella.'

He abandoned the pavement and looked up

at me, and answered in his own tongue also. 'And is the love upon Cordaella for you?'

'Yes,' I said.

'You sound very sure, my fine young Roman Standard-bearer.'

'I am,' I said. 'She told me.'

'And did she tell you that I have already found for her a man of her own people before we left Lindum?'

'Yes, with thirty head of cattle.'

'You, I am thinking, do not have thirty head of cattle. And yet you would be marrying with the girl in his stead.'

'I would!' I said. 'But I cannot – not yet anyway.'

'And why would that be?' said he, with his red brows quirking up towards the roots of his hair.

'In the Legions, no one below the rank of Centurion—'

'Is allowed to take a wife, ah yes. And so you will be needing promotion before she grows weary of waiting. Well – good luck to you, noble Standard-bearer.'

Suddenly I began to feel a flicker of hope.

'You mean – you'll not force her to go to this other man?'

'Force Cordaella?' he said. 'In all the years

93

since our father died, I have never found the
way to make Cordaella do anything she was set
against. If ever you do marry her, it may be that
you will find the way, but I very much doubt it.
Far more likely it will be the other way round!'

'I'll risk it,' I said; and all at once it was as
though the sun came out.

And then the trumpet sounded from the fort,
and I knew that I must be getting back.

CHAPTER THREE

Campaign in the North

.

Later the same day I was standing before the piled writing-table in the Headquarters Office, where Dexius Valens the Senior Centurion had sent for me, waiting for him to notice that I was there. After a while he looked up from the scatter of tablets and papyrus rolls before him, and said, 'Ah, Standard-bearer. – Yes, the General Agricola is at Corstopitum overseeing the arrangements for this summer's Caledonian Campaign. The order has just come through. – We march to join him in three days.'

So that was that. All town leave was stopped, of course, and I never even got to see Cordaella to say farewell to her. Couldn't write her a note, either, because of course she couldn't read anyway. The best I could do was to scratch a few lines to Vedrix and ask him to read them to her – I thought I could trust him – and get one of

the mule-drivers to take the letter down into the town the next day.

And three days later, leaving the usual holding-garrison behind us, we marched out for Corstopitum.

A Legion on the march – that's something worth the seeing; the long winding column, cohort after cohort, the cavalry wings spread on either side and the baggage train following after. A great serpent of mailed men, red-hackled with the crests of the officers' helmets, and whistling whatever tune best pleases them at the moment – 'Payday' perhaps, or 'The Emperor's Wineskins', or 'The Girl I kissed at Clusium', to keep the marching time. Four miles to the hour, never slower, never faster, uphill and down, twenty miles a day. . . . And me, marching up at the head, right behind the Legate on his white horse, carrying the great Eagle of the Legion, with the sunlight splintering on its spread wings; and its talons clutched on the lighting-jags of Jupiter, and the gilded laurel wreaths of its victories. . . .

Aye, I was the proud one, that day! For I'd seen Cordaella among the crowd that gathered to see us off, and she had seen me and waved to me. And I was through with garrison duty and

going to join the fighting, and win my promotion and maybe make a name for myself and come back with the honours shining on my breast; and all for my girl Cordaella. And my breast swelled as though the honours were already there. – What a bairn I was, what a boy with my head chock-full of dreams of glory, for all the great lion-skin that I wore over my armour, and the size of my hands on the Eagle shaft, and my long legs eating up the Northward miles!

But it was three years and more before we came marching back; and there were times when I came near to forgetting Cordaella for a while, though never quite.

CHAPTER FOUR

Eagle's Egg

We joined Agricola with the Twentieth Legion at Corstopitum, and marched on North across the great Lowland hills until we were joined by the main part of the Second and the Fourteenth that had come up through the western country of last summer's campaigning. Then we headed on for the broad Firth that all but cuts Caledonia in half. The Fleet met us there, and we spent the rest of the summer making a naval base. You need something of that sort for supplies, and support, when you can't be sure of your land lines of communication behind you. We saw a bit of fighting from time to time, but seemingly the Lowland chiefs were still too busy fighting with each other, to make a strong show against us, so mostly it was just building; first the supply base, and then with the winter scarce past, a string of turf and timber forts right across the low-lying narrows of the land.

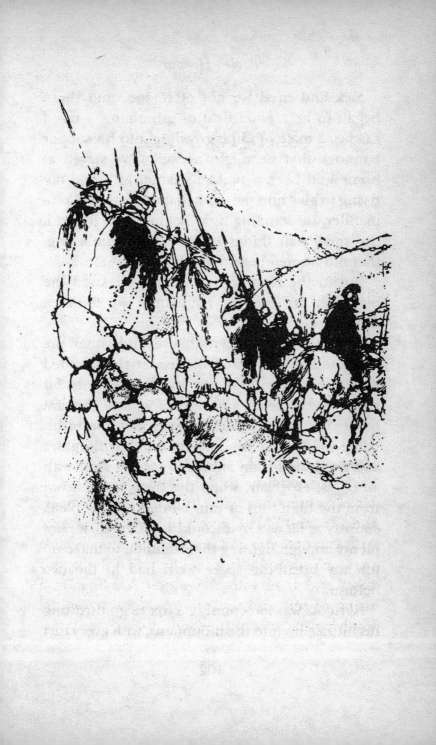

Sick and tired we got of it, too, and there began to be a good deal of grumbling. I mind Lucius, a mate of mine growling into his supper bannock that he might as well have stayed at home and been a builder's labourer – and me trying to give him the wink that the Cohort Commander was standing right behind him. It's odd, the small daft things not worth remembering, that one remembers across half a lifetime. . . .

But in the next spring, when we started the big push on into the Highlands, we found a difference.

Somehow, sometime in that second winter, the Caledonians had found the leader they needed to hammer them into one people. Calgacus, his name was, I never saw him, not until the last battle; but I got so that the bare mention of his name would have me looking over my shoulder and reaching for my sword. It was the same with all of us, especially when the mists came down from the high tops or rain blotted out the bleak country as far as a man could see. Oh yes, we saw plenty enough fighting that summer, to make up for any breathing space we'd had in the two before.

Agricola was too cunning a fox to go thrusting his muzzle up into the mountains, with every turf

of bog-cotton seemingly a war-painted warrior in disguise, waiting to close the glens like a trap on his tail. Instead, he closed them himself, with great forts in the mouths of each one where it came down to the eastern plain. That way, there was no risk of the tribes swarming down unchecked to take us in the rear or cut our supply lines after we had passed by.

We got sullen-sick of fort building, all over again, yes; especially with our shoulder-blades always on the twitch for an arrow between them. The Ninth wintered at Inchtuthil, the biggest of the forts. The place was not finished, but we sat in the middle and went on building it round us, which is never a very comfortable state of things, in enemy country. We lost a lot of men in one way and another; and the old ugly talk of the Ninth being an unlucky Legion woke up and began to drift round again. It might have been better if the Legate had not had a convenient bout of stomach trouble and gone south to winter in Corstopitum. I didn't envy Senior Centurion Dexius left in command. It was our third winter in the wilds, and we were sick of snow and hill mists, and the painted devils sniping at us from behind every gorse-bush; and we wanted to be able to drink with our friends in a wine

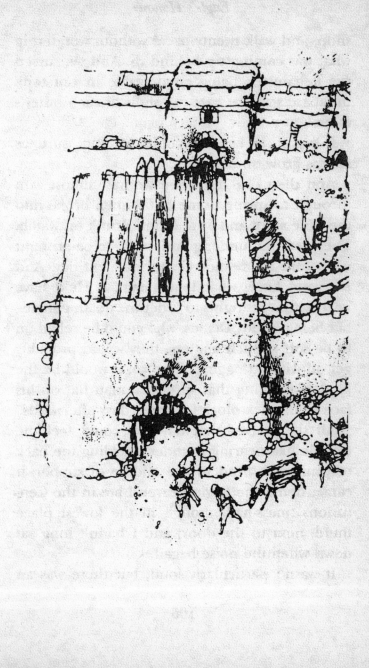

shop, and walk twenty paces without wondering what was coming up behind us. And we cursed the Legate for being comfortable in Corstopitum, and grew to hate the sight of each other's faces.

I began to smell trouble coming, sure as acorns grow on oak trees.

And then one day when we had almost won through to spring, some of the men broke into the wine store and were found drunk on watch. They were put under guard, ready to be brought up before the Senior Centurion next day. And everyone knew what that meant. – He'd have been within his rights to order the death penalty; but being Daddy Dexius, who could be relied on to be soft in such matters, they would probably get off with a flogging. Even so, it would be the kind of flogging that spreads a man flat on his face in the sick block for three days afterwards.

All the rest of that day you could feel the trouble like nearing thunder prickling the back of your neck. And in the middle of supper, it came. Being the Eagle Bearer, I ate in the Centurions' mess-hall, though in the lowest place there, next to the door; and I hadn't long sat down when the noise began.

It wasn't particularly loud, but there was an

ugly note to it; a snarling note; 'Come on, lads, let's get the prisoners out!' and other voices taking up the cry.

I remember Dexius's face as he got up and strode past me to the door; and suddenly knowing that we had all been quite wrong about him; that he wasn't soft at all. – More the kind of man who gets a reputation for being good-tempered and fair-game, because he knows that if he once lets his temper go and hits somebody he probably won't leave off till he's killed them.

I had only just started my supper, so I snatched a hard-boiled duck's egg from a bowl on the table and shoved it down the front of my uniform, and dashed out with the rest.

Outside on the parade-ground a crowd was gathering. Some of them had makeshift torches. The flare of them was teased by the thin wind that was blowing, and their light fell ragged on faces that were sullen and dangerous. Vipsanius the duty centurion was trying to deal with the situation, but he didn't seem to be having much success, and the crowd was getting bigger every moment.

Daddy Dexius said coolly, 'What goes on here, Centurion?'

'They're refusing to go on watch, Sir,' said

Vipsanius. I mind he was sweating up a bit, despite the edge to the wind.

'We've had enough of going on watch in this dog-hole, night after filthy night!' someone shouted.

And his mates backed him up. 'How much longer are we going to squat here, making a free target of ourselves for the blue painted barbarians?'

'If Agricola wants to fight them, why doesn't he come up and get things going?'

'Otherwise why don't we get out of here and go back where we came from?'

Men began shouting from all over the crowd, bringing up all the old soldiers' grievances about pay and leave and living conditions. 'We've had enough!' they shouted. 'We've had enough!'

'You'll have had more than enough, and the Painted People down on us, if you don't break up and get back on duty!' Vipsanius yelled back at them.

But the sullen crowd showed no sign of breaking up or getting back, on duty. And suddenly, only half-believing, I understood just how ugly things might be going to turn. Not much harm done up to now, but if something, anything, tipped matters even a little in the wrong

direction, the whole crowd could flare up into revolt, and a revolt has a way of spreading that puts a heath-fire to shame.

Centurion Dexius said, 'Thank you, Centurion, I will take over now.' And then he glanced round for me. 'Standard-bearer.'

'Here, Sir,' says I, advancing smartly.

'Go and fetch out the Eagle, and we'll see if that will bring them to their senses.'

I left him standing there, not trying to shout them down or anything, just standing there, and went to fetch the Eagle.

In the Saccellum, part office and part treasury and part shrine, the lamp was burning on the table where the duty centurion would sit all night with his drawn sword before him – when not doing Rounds or out trying to quell a riot – and the Eagle on its tall shaft stood against the wall, with the Cohort standards ranged on either side of it.

I took it down; and as I did so its upward shadow, cast by the lamp on the table engulfed half the chamber behind it, as though some vast dark bird had spread wing and come swooping forward out of the gloom among the rafters. Used though I was to the Eagle standard, that great swoop of dark wings made me jump half out of my skin. But it was not the moment to be having fancies. I hitched up the Eagle into Parade Position, and out I went with it.

The Senior Centurion had quieted them down a bit; well, the look on his face would have quieted all Rome on a feast day; and when they saw the Eagle, their growling and muttering died away till I could hear a fox barking, way up the glen, and the vixen's scream in answer. But they still stood their ground, and I knew the quiet wouldn't last. And there was I, standing up with the Eagle, not knowing quite what to do next; and truth to tell, beginning to feel a bit of a fool. And then suddenly it came to me; what I had to do next; and I pulled out the duck's egg from inside my tunic and held it up.

And, 'Now look what you've done, you lot!' said I. 'Behaving like this you've upset the Eagle so much its laid an egg!'

I have noticed more than once in the years since then, that it is sometimes easier to swing the mood of a whole crowd than it is to swing the mood of one man on his own. Aye, a dicey thing is a crowd.

There was a moment of stunned silence, and then someone laughed, and someone else took up the laugh, and then more and more, a roar

of laughter and a surge of stamping and back-
slapping that swept away all that had gone
before.

CHAPTER FIVE

The Last Battle

And so we were still in Inchtuthil, and more or less in one piece, when the Legate came back to us, fat and prosperous as a moneylender after his winter in Corstopitum. And then Agricola came up from the Naval Base with the rest of the army, and as soon as the grass stood high enough to feed the cavalry horses, the advance was on again.

It was not easy going. No set-piece battles, but we had to fight for every hill pass and river ford; arrows came at us from every thicket, and once, the Painted Men fired the forest ahead of us when the wind was blowing our way. But at last, a weary long while it seemed since we marched from Inchtuthil, we came up towards the first dark wave-lift of the Grampians. – They call the place Mons Graupius, now; it hadn't got a name then; at least it hadn't got a name in our tongue, it just seemed like the world's end. – And we

116

had word back from the scouts that we had sent way up ahead, that Calgacus was waiting for us among the wooded gullies of the lower slopes, the whole Caledonian war-host with him.

Agricola halted the Legions, and gave orders for the usual war camp to be pitched.

The great square was measured out, and the banks and stockades thrown up; the General's pavilion set up in the midst of all, with the tents of the Legates on either side, and the Eagles of the four Legions ranged in front. The camp fires, one to each fifty men, were built in long straight rows, and the horse-lines and baggage park pegged out in position; the guards were posted and a meal of hard bannock and sour wine issued to all of us, and we settled in for the night.

But the nights are short in the north at that time of year, and it was morning soon enough, and Caledonians and Romans alike stirring for battle.

Tacitus, Agricola's son-in-law, who wrote a history of that campaign later, sets down a fine fiery dawn-of-battle speech for Calgacus. I learned it almost by heart, in after years, for it's a good speech though not over polite to us Romans.

Something like this, it went: 'My brothers, – this I bid you to remember when the war horns sound: there is nothing beyond us but the sea; and even on the sea the galleys of the Red Crests prowl like wolf packs. Therefore there can be no retreat for us, we conquer or we die. And we shall conquer! The Roman victories came not by their strength but by our weakness, and our weakness was that we were many Tribes divided among ourselves. Now we stand together as one People, and we are strong! They are fewer in number than we, they are strangers under strange skies; the mountains and the forests are enemies to them and friends to us. . . . My brothers, we have this choice: victory at whatever cost, and freedom, or the Roman yoke upon our necks, our women enslaved, our young men carried off to serve the Romans at the other end of the world! We have heard of the Roman Peace, but in truth, they make a desolation and call it Peace! Keep that in your hearts as you rush into battle!'

Aye, a good rabble-rousing speech. – Though come to think of it, I wonder how Tacitus knew what he said, or if he said anything like that at all.

I do know what Agricola said, for I heard him,

when he harangued us, standing on a tub of arrowheads.

'Comrades,' says he, 'we have fought through more than one campaign together. I think that you have been content with your General; I know that I have been well enough satisfied with my soldiers.' (I thought about the Eagle and the egg!) 'We have pushed on further than all other of our armies, and here we stand in the farthest part of Britain, where never any man carried the Eagles before. But though the land is strange to us, the men we fight today are the same as those we fought and routed and forced back in earlier time. They ran then, and they'll run again; it is because they are so good at running that they have lasted so long. So now, lads – one good sharp heave for the glory of old Mother Rome, and the thing is done!'

And we cheered him until our cheering echoed back from the dark woods and the mountain corries.

Well then, our battle line was drawn up, the lightly armed foot-soldiers of the auxiliary cohorts in the centre, the cavalry on the wings, and the heavy troops of the Legions drawn up behind, along the line of last night's banks and ditches. The Ninth was held in reserve, and we

didn't think much of that, but it's a job some-body has to do.

That was my first full-pitched battle, and I'll not be forgetting it in a hurry. I'll not be forget-ting the great wave of the Caledonian chariot charge thundering down upon our battle line; and the way our line swayed and bulged a bit, but held firm, and the charge broke, like a wave breaking on rocks, and curled back on itself. Our lads charged forward after them; and it was then that Calgacus sent in a second charge, sweeping down from the hills and circling wide to take our battle-mass from the rear. It was red and ancient chaos after that, though the cavalry did their job finely, and the banks and ditches of the camp itself played a useful part in throw-ing the Caledonian chariots into confusion. Aye, a bad patch, and they all but crumpled up our left wing, and for a while the battle could have gone either way. It was six cohorts of the Ninth, pushed up from the reserve to thicken the battle line, that saved the situation and held it, steady as a rock, while the Fourteenth had a chance to re-form and rally to their own Eagle. The old Ninth has come on evil days since then, but I shan't forget that, either; the spread wings of our Eagle bright in sunlight, and the Roman

battle-mass staggering and then growing steady again, and thrusting forward. . . .

The fighting began a little after sun-up; and before the sun stood at noon the Caledonian war-host was a broken rabble, being hunted through their forests and across their heather moors by us victorious Romans. At nightfall the hunt was called off, for it is not good to hunt even a broken enemy through strange country in the dark. And when the moon rose, it shone down – have you ever noticed how coldly uncaring the moon can seem? – on smashed chariots and dead horses, and dead men among the blood-sodden heather.

That was when I saw Calgacus; the only time. I saw him by the cold moonlight, lying at the foot of the slope where the fighting had been heaviest, with the finest of his warriors about him, and his long hair tangled into the roots of a pale flowered bramble bush.

Our losses were officially put at three hundred and sixty, including Valarius, a Centurion of the Ninth, and one young fool of a Tribune who rode right into a rear-guard fight at the edge of the woods. The Caledonians lost thousands; more than half their war-host, besides those that were taken captive.

Calgacus had staked everything, the whole fighting strength of Caledonia, on that last battle; and when it was over the war in Caledonia was over too.

Three days later the Senior Centurion sent for me to his tent. He was rubbing his chin with a piece of pumice when I went in. – He was one of the few soldiers I have known who always contrived to keep a smooth chin even on campaign. – And he laid down the pumice and felt his jaw enquiringly for traces of a beard.

'I am promoting Centurion Gaurus to Centurion Valarius's place. You will take over Gaurus's century,' he said. Just like that!

'Sir,' I said. I felt a bit winded. And yet truth to tell, I wasn't altogether surprised. Somebody was due for promotion, with Valarius having got himself killed, and I knew I'd done well in the battle. I suppose I puffed my chest out a bit.

And suddenly he laughed, 'And you can take that smirk off your face. You carried out your duties extremely well when the Painted Men nearly crumpled up our left wing; in fact one might say with courage and devotion; but Roma Dea! What else do you think the Legions expect of their standard-bearers? That business about the Eagle and the egg, now, I'm not at all sure

128

it wasn't disrespect to the Gods, but it ended a very nasty situation, and showed that you have the trick of handling men. Go and take over from Gaurus. – Oh, wait—' and he picked up a roughly trimmed hazel stick, – we'd hacked down a bit of hazel and thorn scrub when we were clearing the ground for the camp – and tossed it to me. 'This will serve you for your vine-staff until we get back to Eburacum and it can be changed for the proper thing. Your promotion will have to be confirmed then, too, but I think you need not worry about that. Lucius will take over from you as Eagle-bearer.'

And he picked up his bit of pumice again and got back to work on his chin.

CHAPTER SIX

Return to Eburacum

It was late into the autumn when the Ninth came marching back into Eburacum, and the crowds gathered to watch us in as they had gathered to watch us march out, more than three years ago; but I could see no sign of Cordaella among them. Not that you can look about you over-much when you're on the march. I told myself that was why I had missed her, and there was no need to be anxious. But of course I was anxious all the same; and the first instant that I could get town leave, I was off to look for her.

But passing the Camp Commandant's house on the way to the Main Gate, I was pulled up short by a familiar sound; the small sharp 'Tip-tip-tap' of a light hammer and chisel cutting the tiny squares for a picture-floor. I knew that sound too well to be mistaken in it. At any rate Vedrix had not gone back to Lindum.

I doubled round a corner and through a side

door, following my ears, as you might say, and across a small courtyard beyond, and finally ran Vedrix himself to ground, squatting amid his little cubes of chalk and sandstone and brick and shale, in what looked like a new bath-house sticking out from the Camp Commandant's quarters.

He looked up, grinning that foxy grin of his, when I appeared.

'Good morning to you, Centurion.'

'You know then,' I said, stopping in my tracks.

'One hears these things.'

I sketched him a kind of mock salute. 'Centurion, Sixth Century, Ninth Cohort. That's about the lowest form of life in the Centurions' Mess.' And then my anxiety caught up with me, and I burst out in a rush, 'But it does mean that I can marry now, if – if – ' and I couldn't bring out the last bit at all.

'If Cordaella hasn't changed her mind?' said Vedrix.

'How is it with Cordaella? Three years is a long time.'

'It was all well with her less than an hour ago. But three years is a long time, even as you say; and maybe you had best go and ask her herself, before it gets any longer.'

'I'll be doing that!' I said, and departed without waiting to take my leave.

I had to pass quite close to the well where I had first spoken to her, to reach her house; but I think I would have gone that way even if it had been a round about journey. I had a feeling. . . .

And there she was, her red hair lighting up the grey little street, just as I remembered. She had filled the pail and set it on the well curb beside her. And she was just sitting there, half-turned to gaze down into the water. She looked somehow as though she had been sitting there quite a while.

But she did not look up when I came along the street; not till I was standing right beside her.

'That pail is much too heavy for a little bird like you,' I said. 'Let me carry it home for you.'

She looked up then, as I reached for the pail; and next instant it wasn't the pail that I had hold of, it was Cordaella, and she had her arms round my neck and was half laughing and half crying and clinging on to me as though she never wanted to let go. And I – well I won't say I wasn't doing my share of the hugging, too.

'I didn't see you when we marched in

yesterday,' I said. 'Why did you not come out with everybody else to see us marching back?'

'I was so afraid,' she said.

'Afraid?'

She nodded against my shoulder. 'That when the Eagle came up the street, I would not see you there.'

'Well I'd not have been carrying the Eagle, but you would have seen me at the head of my Cohort,' I said. 'Cordaella, I have my vine staff now.'

'I know,' she said. 'We heard later. Quintus, I am so proud of you!'

I wanted to boast a bit, seem big in her eyes; but I've never been a very good liar. 'I didn't get it for being a hero,' I told her. 'I got it for making a bad joke at the right moment.'

'We heard about that, too,' she said, soft with laughter. And then she suddenly turned grave, and held me off at arms' length, and stood looking at me. 'I do not believe that your great strong Roman Legions that march about in straight lines and build square forts would ever choose their Centurions just for making jokes at the right moment,' she said. 'But anyhow, I am thinking that people who make bad jokes at the

right moment are maybe much easier to be mar-
ried to, than heroes.'

Within a year, Agricola had been recalled to
Rome, and the whole Fourteenth Legion had
been pulled out from Britain to strengthen the
German Frontier. That meant that Inchtuthil
and all the Northern forts had to be abandoned; and almost the whole campaign was
wasted. But that's the way it is with armies on
the frontiers and governments at home. . . .

Well, there you are. At any rate it got me
my first Century, and you younglings a British
grandmother.

Throw another log on the fire.

Other great reads ✧ *from* **Red Fox**

Further Red Fox titles that you might enjoy reading are listed on the following pages. They are available in bookshops or they can be ordered directly from us.

If you would like to order books, please send this form and the money due to:

ARROW BOOKS, BOOKSERVICE BY POST, PO BOX 29, DOUGLAS, ISLE OF MAN, BRITISH ISLES. Please enclose a cheque or postal order made out to Arrow Books Ltd for the amount due, plus 75p per book for postage and packing to a maximum of £7.50, both for orders within the UK. For customers outside the UK, please allow £1.00 per book.

NAME_____

ADDRESS_____

_____

Please print clearly.

Whilst every effort is made to keep prices low, it is sometimes necessary to increase cover prices at short notice. If you are ordering books by post, to save delay it is advisable to phone to confirm the correct price. The number to ring is THE SALES DEPARTMENT 071 (if outside London) 973 9700.

Other great reads ✦ *from* **Red Fox**

Superb historical stories from Rosemary Sutcliff

Rosemary Sutcliff tells the historical story better than anyone else. Her tales are of times filled with high adventure, desperate enterprises, bloody encounters and tender romance. Discover the vividly real world of Rosemary Sutcliff today!

THE CAPRICORN BRACELET
ISBN 0 09 977620 0   £2.50

KNIGHT'S FEE
ISBN 0 09 977630 8   £2.99

THE SHINING COMPANY
ISBN 0 09 985580 1   £3.50

THE WITCH'S BRAT
ISBN 0 09 975080 5   £2.50

SUN HORSE, MOON HORSE
ISBN 0 09 979550 7   £2.50

TRISTAN AND ISEULT
ISBN 0 09 979550 7   £2.99

BEOWULF: DRAGON SLAYER
ISBN 0 09 997270 0   £2.50

THE HOUND OF ULSTER
ISBN 0 09 997260 3   £2.99

THE LIGHT BEYOND THE FOREST
ISBN 0 09 997450 9   £2.99

THE SWORD AND THE CIRCLE
ISBN 0 09 997460 6   £2.99

Gripping Red Fox Fiction for Older Readers

BETWEEN THE MOON AND THE ROCK
Judy Allen

Shy Lisa feels that she has finally found a voice when she joins the Christian fundamental group that have recently moved in next door – but her best friend Flora feels that there is something frighteningly evil behind their mesmerising services.

ISBN 0 09 918651 9   £2.99

TINA COME HOME
Paul Geraghty

New to England, Murray is fascinated by Tina, the most unusual, interesting girl he's ever met. Not daring to approach her, he starts secretly trailing her home from school . . . which is when he stumbles upon her secret.

ISBN 0 09 971710 7   £3.50

PAUL LOVES AMY LOVES CHRISTO
Josephine Poole

Paul and his sister Amy have always been the greatest friends, and he takes it for granted that he is the most important person in her life. When she falls in love, his whole world is suddenly shattered, and he has to face the violence of his emotions.

ISBN 0 09 974040 0   £3.50

YOU'LL NEVER GUESS THE END
Barbara Wersba

Joel's black sheep brother has hit the bestseller lists with a novel Joel knows is rubbish. Life's not fair, and it's beginning to get him down – until a bizarre chain of events lead Joel into the spotlight . . .

ISBN 0 09 911381 3   £3.50

Top teenage fiction from Red Fox

PLAY NIMROD FOR HIM   Jean Ure
Christopher and Nick are each other's only friend.
Isolated from the rest of the crowd, they live in their
own world of writing and music. Enter lively, popular
Sal who tempts Christopher away from Nick . . .
ISBN 0 09 985300 0   £2.99

HAMLET, BANANAS AND ALL THAT JAZZ
Alan Durant
Bert, Jim and their mates vow to live dangerously –
just as Nietzsche said. So starts a post-GCSEs summer
of girls, parties, jazz, drink, fags . . . and tragedy.
ISBN 0 09 997540 8   £3.50

ENOUGH IS TOO MUCH ALREADY
Jan Mark
Maurice, Nina and Nazzer are all re-sitting their
O levels but prefer to spend their time musing over
hilarious previous encounters with strangers, hamsters,
wild parties and Japanese radishes . . .
ISBN 0 09 985310 8   £2.99

BAD PENNY   Allan Frewin Jones
Christmas doesn't look good for Penny this year. She's
veggy, feels overweight, *and* The Lizard, her horrible
father has just turned up. Worse still, Roy appears –
Penny's ex whom she took a year to get over.
ISBN 0 09 985280 2   £2.99

CUTTING LOOSE   Carole Lloyd
Charlie's horoscope says to get back into the swing of
things, but it's not easy: her Dad and Gran aren't
speaking, she's just found out the truth about her
mum, and is having severe confused spells about her
lovelife. It's time to cut loose from all binding ties, and
decide what she wants and who she really is.
ISBN 0 09 91381 X   £3.50